# Little Ant and the Grasshopper

## S.M.R. Saia

Illustrations by Tina Perko

It was the height of summer. The world was full of food, and Little Ant and his brother ants were busy all the time, bringing it back to the anthill.

The grasshoppers, though, did not gather or store food. They spent their time singing and dancing and enjoying the sunshine.

"We all enjoy your music," Little Ant said to the grasshopper one day. "But aren't you worried about the winter?"

"There is plenty of food on the ground and plenty of time to gather it," the grasshopper said. "We grasshoppers have shows to put on every day this week. We are too busy to gather food right now."

"But every insect has to gather food," Little Ant replied. Other ants, who were nearby, agreed.

The grasshopper's usually cheerful face became long and sad, and he hung his head. He knew — every insect in the field knew — that they were supposed to gather food for the winter. But the grasshopper did not like lifting and carrying, and he was not very good at it.

The summer went by, and the grasshoppers did not gather much food. They sang and danced and played music for anyone who would stop to listen, and they enjoyed themselves very much indeed.

One day, Little Ant asked his friend if he and the other grasshoppers were ready for winter. "We have stored up some food," the grasshopper told him nervously, "but it's not enough. I work very hard on my songs and my dances," he continued, "but working like an ant makes me feel miserable."

Little Ant thought about what his friend had said. He had not known that the grasshoppers worked on their songs and dances, which looked so easy.

Little Ant liked his friend, but he felt he was being foolish. There was only one kind of work that mattered in the summer and only one way to survive the winter. The days were getting shorter and cooler and darker, and there was no time to waste.

Soon the cold began to bite, and the ants settled in for the winter. When the grasshoppers had eaten all of the food that they had, they came to the anthill to ask for help.

"You should have worked all summer, like we did," the ants told the grasshoppers. "If you were more like ants, then you wouldn't be hungry."

The ants had plenty to eat, but they were not happy. They missed being able to leave the anthill to look for food. Some spent hours in the storeroom every day, counting crumbs and seeds. Others took naps. Still others began to grumble and argue. Little Ant, who loved to lift and go out looking for food, was bored, and spring was still a very, very long way away.

One day, Little Ant thought of his friend the grasshopper. "We should put on a show," he suggested to some of the other ants. "We could sing and dance and entertain the whole anthill."

Every ant, at one time or another, had idled in the summer sunshine to watch the grasshoppers. The others agreed that a show would be just the thing to cheer everybody up.

They split up into groups to put together acts. Little Ant and Buddy Ant decided to do a dance. But it turned out that dancing was not as easy as it looked.

"You're not doing it right," Little Ant complained.

"Stop stepping on my feet!" Buddy Ant cried.

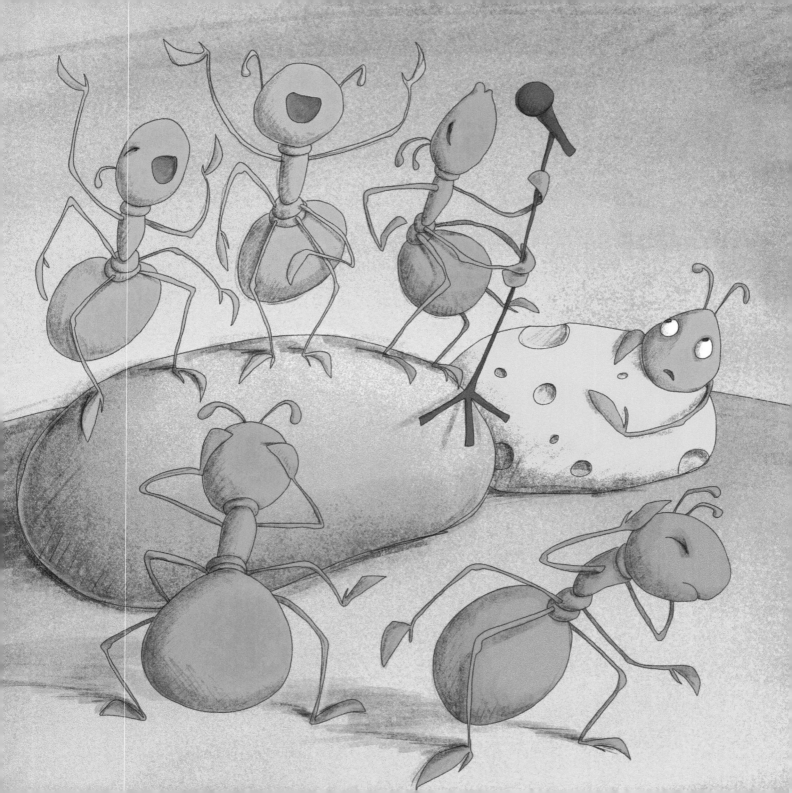

Some of the ants wanted to sing in the show. But it soon became clear that ants could not sing as well as grasshoppers. In fact, ants could not sing at all.

"No one is going to want to see this show," Buddy Ant said. Little Ant agreed. Plus, the ants were finding that they did not enjoy singing and dancing all day long. They did not enjoy organizing shows. One by one they crept away to do other things. They went back to grumbling, and arguing, and waiting for the seemingly endless winter to end.

One day, the grasshoppers came begging again and were again sent away. Every ant who heard about it agreed that ants were far superior to grasshoppers. All — that is — except for Little Ant. He thought about how hard it was to sing and dance, and how difficult it had been to put on a show.

"Ants love to lift, and we love to go out looking for food. But my friend the grasshopper is not an ant," Little Ant said to Buddy Ant. "So why do we think he ought to act like one?"

"Everybody is saying that the grasshoppers deserve to be hungry because they did not work in the summer," Buddy Ant replied. "But I loved watching the grasshoppers sing and dance. I would give a whole crumb if I could see a grasshopper show right now."

"Buddy Ant!" Little Ant cried. "That's a great idea!"

"What idea?" Buddy Ant said, as Little Ant turned and scurried off down a tunnel.

Not far from his anthill, Little Ant found the grasshoppers. He gave them some crumbs to eat. Then he said, "We have plenty of food in the anthill, but we are bored and restless. If we pay you in seeds and crumbs, will you come to the anthill every day and perform for us?"

The grasshoppers were delighted to agree.

The grasshoppers entertained the ants in exchange for food every day for the rest of the winter. They were happy to be appreciated — at last — for being grasshoppers. They worked hard on their shows, and each one was better than the one before. That winter, nobody was bored, unhappy, or hungry.

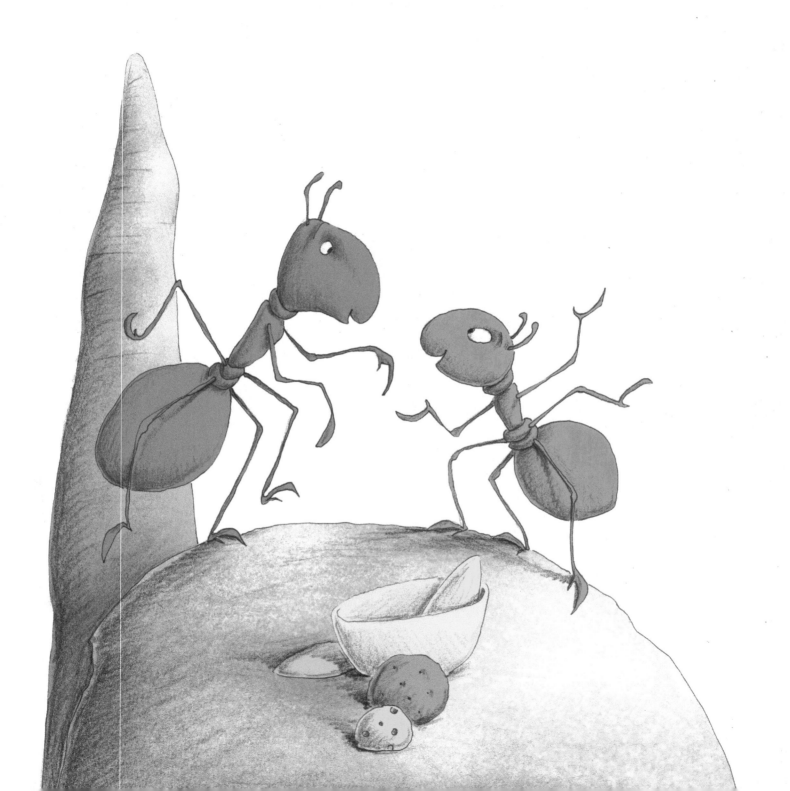

"You have done a good thing, Little Ant," Uncle Ant said, "for the grasshoppers and the ants."

"I am happy for my friend the grasshopper," Little Ant replied. "And he has taught me a valuable lesson."

"What's that?" Uncle Ant asked.

"If you choose a job that you love," Little Ant replied, "You will never have to work a day in your life."

Free activities for the Little Ant books are available at
http://littleantbooks.com.

Follow Little Ant on Facebook and Instagram at @littleantnews. Learn more about
Little Ant's life; be the first to know when there are new Little Ant activities available
for free download, and get cool news about insects you can share with your kids!

Published by Shelf Space Books
http://shelfspacebooks.com

ISBN: 978-1-945713-36-1